For Olivia xx – LR

To Rara and Pounce for always
believing in my creativity – TRB

Published in the UK by Scholastic, 2025
1 London Bridge, London, SE1 9BG
Scholastic Ireland, 89E Lagan Road, Dublin Industrial Estate, Glasnevin, Dublin, D11 HP5F

ISBN 978 0702 32254 9

A CIP catalogue record for this book is available from the British Library.

Printed in China
Paper made from wood grown in sustainable forests and other controlled sources.

1 3 5 7 9 10 8 6 4 2

www.scholastic.co.uk

Lucy Rowland

Tilia Rand-Bell

Unicorn Babies

SCHOLASTIC

The Unicorn Babies were the very best of friends.
They lived beside the river where the magic rainbow ends.

There was
Pinky.

There was Inky.

There was one called Little Bea.

And they all played in the meadow by the sleepy willow tree.

Their days were full of sunshine.
Fluffy clouds as white as snow.

Bright flowers filled the meadow
and the river seemed to glow.

But one day, as the unicorns were playing all together, they peered up at the sky and wondered,

"WHAT'S THAT FUNNY WEATHER?"

For over in the distance,
where the white clouds met the sun,

They saw some new, **much darker**
clouds that didn't look so fun.

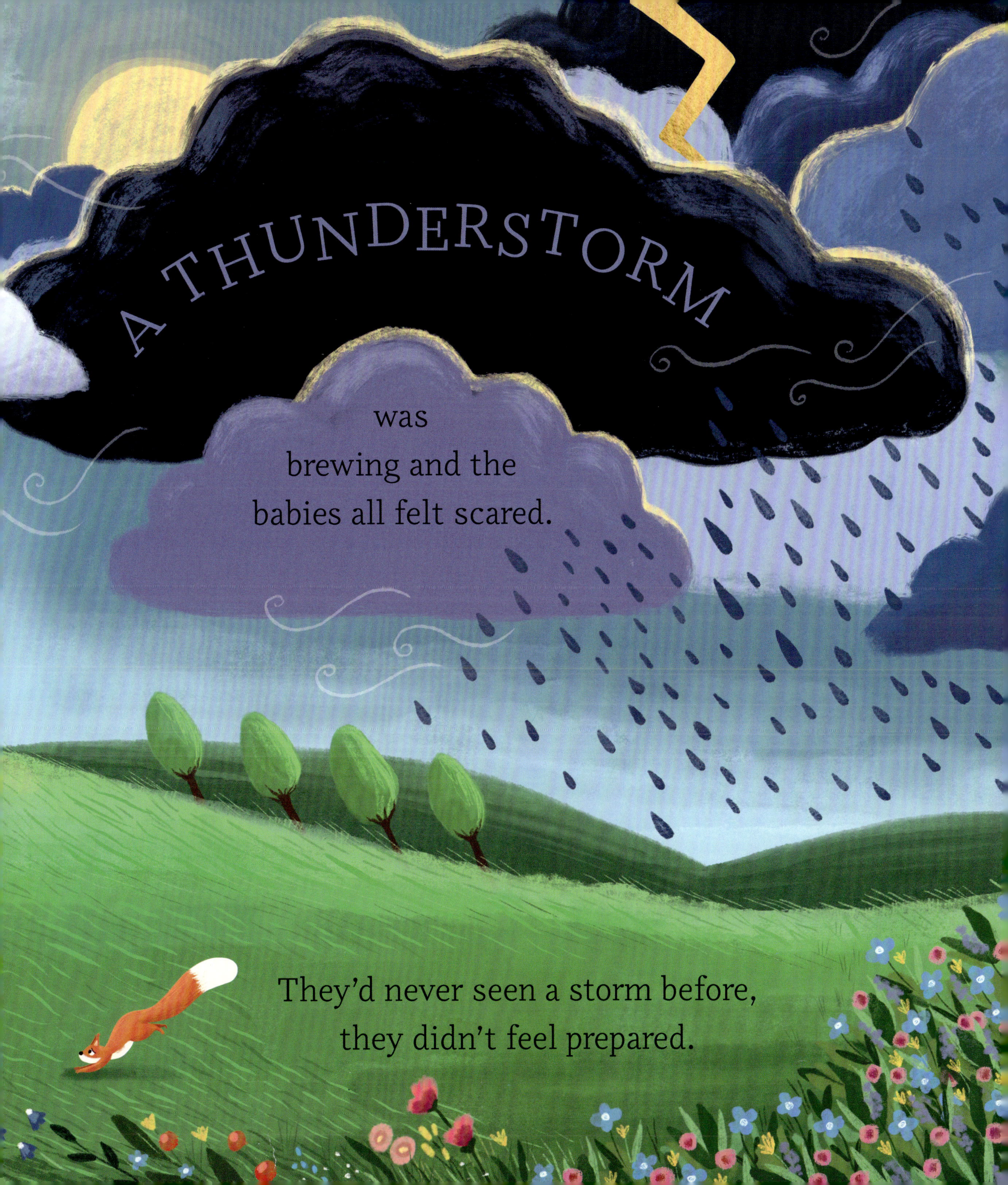

A THUNDERSTORM

was
brewing and the
babies all felt scared.

They'd never seen a storm before,
they didn't feel prepared.

The sky grew dark as night drew in.
The storm was getting near.

"I don't like dark!"
poor Pinky gasped.

Her eyes were
wide with fear.

But Inky whispered gently,
"Dark is beautiful and fun!
You can't see stars without
the dark. Dark's just as
good as sun!"

"I bet you any
minute that those
clouds will part . . ."
And soon,
they felt a little
brighter as they
saw the shiny moon.

But then, the wind picked up again.
There came a blinding **FLASH!**

"Oh no! It's noisy!" Inky cried,
as thunder **BOOMED**
and **CRASHED.**

But then Bea had a good
idea and gave a tiny grin.

"Let's sing a song!
Drown out the
noise! I'll start
and you join in!"

The babies sang together and the thunderbolts were loud.

But their song was even louder as they sang up to the clouds.

And soon they didn't feel afraid . . .
Till . . . branches overhead,

Waved spooky shadows on the floor . . .

"A MONSTER," poor Bea said.

"A very
SCARY
monster!"

and she gave
a little yelp.

Then Pinky thought,
"Poor Little Bea,"
and knew she
had to help.

"I'll show you there's no monster.
You'll be fine. Just wait right here."

Then Pinky stepped into the night (with just a hint of fear).

"THERE'S NO SUCH THING AS MONSTERS!"

And quite soon they'd see for certain!
The willow branches parted and then
closed, just like a curtain.

But outside it seemed darker still.
Clouds drifted past the moon.

Without her two friends singing,
Pinky heard the thunder

BOOM!

Those spooky shadows moved and swayed ...
and were they getting **nearer?**

A monster's hand?
A monster's face?

The shapes
were getting
clearer!

So Pinky ran!

Beneath her hooves, the rain soon turned to frost.

She shivered. "Time to go back home." But, oh no . . . she was . . .

lost!

"I wonder where our willow is,
and where the rainbow ends . . ."

Then Pinky gave
a little sniff,
"Wherever are my friends?"

Oh! What was that?

Two voices!

And they called,
"Where are you, Pinky?"

Then, as the moon
came out once more . . .

Look!
Little Bea and Inky!

They galloped up to Pinky then

they laughed and hugged - **all three!**

At last, the babies all felt calm.
The storm was passing by.

"Let's get
some sleep,"
yawned Inky,
as he gazed
up to the sky.

But, as the three were drifting off, they heard a noisy …

ROARRR!

Ha! No! Just Pinky's **SNORE!**

The unicorns all giggled,
then they cuddled
close and warm.

Three baby friends together.
They could weather any storm.